# Whirlwind Is a Ghost Dancing

# NATALIA BELTING

## *Whirlwind Is a Ghost Dancing*

illustrated by Leo and Diane Dillon

E. P. DUTTON & CO., INC.  NEW YORK

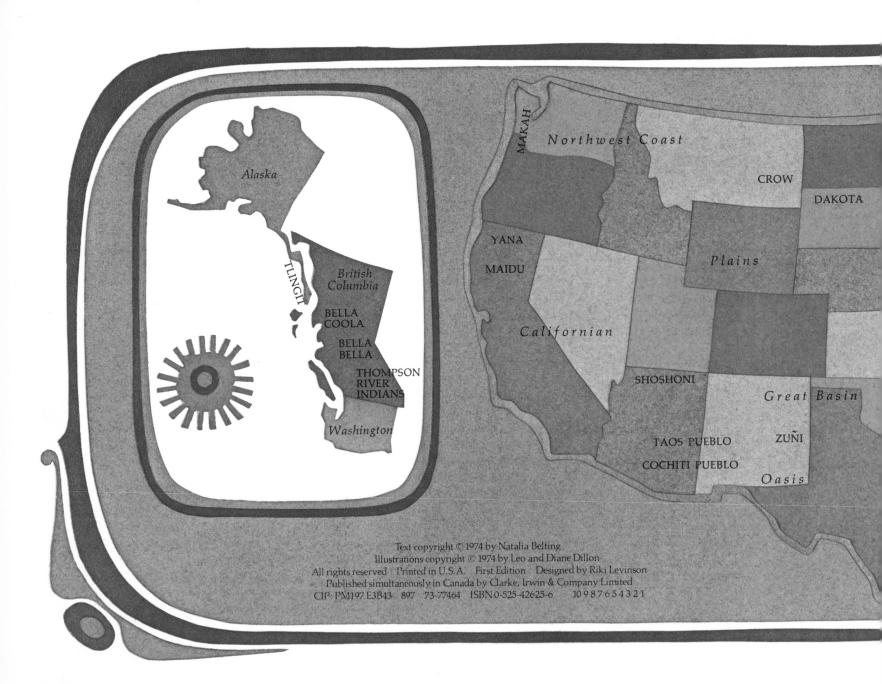

Alaska

TLINGIT

British
Columbia

BELLA
COOLA

BELLA
BELLA

THOMPSON
RIVER
INDIANS

Washington

MAKAH

Northwest Coast

CROW

DAKOTA

YANA

MAIDU

Plains

Californian

SHOSHONI

Great Basin

TAOS PUEBLO

ZUÑI

COCHITI PUEBLO

Oasis

Text copyright © 1974 by Natalia Belting
Illustrations copyright © 1974 by Leo and Diane Dillon
All rights reserved   Printed in U.S.A.   First Edition   Designed by Riki Levinson
Published simultaneously in Canada by Clarke, Irwin & Company Limited
CIP: PM197.E3B43   897   73-77464   ISBN 0-525-42625-6   10 9 8 7 6 5 4 3 2 1

770127

SKIDI PAWNEE

IROQUOIS

*Northeast Woodland*

MICMAC

*New Brunswick*

*Nova Scotia*

*Maine*

*Southeast Woodland*

Wind is a ghost
That whirls and turns,
Twists in fleet moccasins,
Sweeps up dust spinning
Across the dry flatlands.

Whirlwind
Is a ghost dancing.

*Dakota*
NORTH AND
SOUTH DAKOTA

In the beginning there was no earth.
There was only water and Turtle floating about
   on a raft.

One day Earth-Maker dropped down on a rope
   from the sky.
Turtle said to him, "I am tired floating on this raft."

So Earth-Maker cleaned Turtle's nails,
Formed the dirt from them into a flat cake,
Laid it on Turtle's raft.

*Maidu*
CALIFORNIA

The cake stretched out. It grew. It became Earth.
Turtle sat on it and basked.

The sky is a bowl of ice
Turned over above the earth.

The rainbow is a serpent
Rubbing his back against the ice,
Shedding his skin in bits of snow and rain.

*Shoshoni*
NEVADA AND UTAH

A man sits in the ice
Northward from here,
Holds the earth between his outstretched legs
With ropes.

Sometimes the earth slips.
He tightens the ropes to steady it.

For a moment, the earth shakes.

*Bella Coola*
BRITISH COLUMBIA

*Thompson River Indians*
BRITISH COLUMBIA

Moon sits smoking his pipe.
Night after clear night he sits smoking,
And the clouds are the smoke from his pipe.

When rain is coming, or snow,
He lays out a hoop around himself,
A circle of frozen smoke,
Builds a house for himself on its frame,
Sits in the doorway smoking
Until the snow begins, or the rain.

Digger Boy was hunting clams.
He cried because he could not find enough
    to fill his bucket.
"If you do not stop crying, the moon will take
    you away,"
His sister told him. Four times she told him.

Digger Boy cried.

Moon came down, carried him off.
The shadows on the moon are Digger Boy
    with his bucket.

*Bella Bella*
BRITISH COLUMBIA

Dew Eagle, at night,
Comes out of his lodge west of the sun.
He carries a bowl of water on his back
And spreads cooling dew over the hot earth.

*Iroquois*
NEW YORK

Not long after the earth was made
And men and birds and animals came upon it,
The sun traveled low in the sky.
Bear's white coat was burned black,
Grizzly Bear's coat was scorched.

So Earth-Maker's son raised mountains
To fence the sun safely away.

*Bella Coola*
BRITISH COLUMBIA

Before men came up from below the earth
  to live,
The mother of men made the stars;
Made them of cornmeal dough
And did not bake them
So that the cornmeal would shine yellow
  in the sky.

*Cochiti Pueblo*
NEW MEXICO

*Bella Coola*
BRITISH COLUMBIA

Sun rays shining through the dusty air,
Breaking through the rain clouds,
Are Earth-Maker's eyelashes.

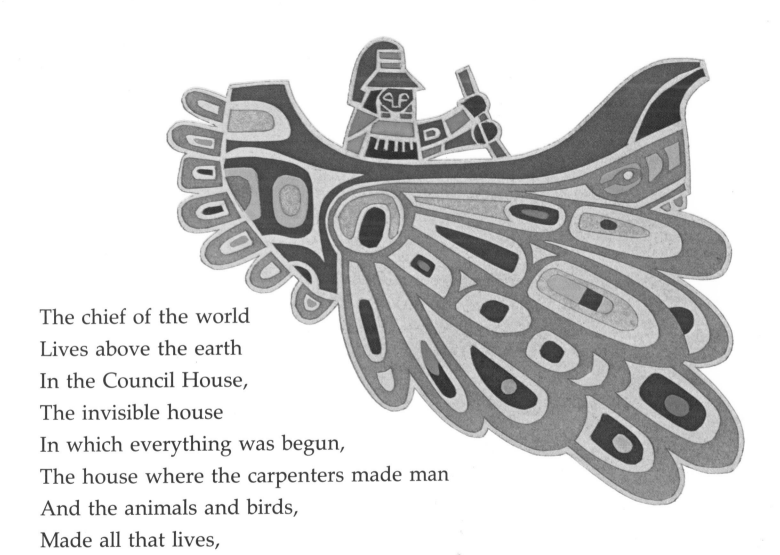

The chief of the world
Lives above the earth
In the Council House,
The invisible house
In which everything was begun,
The house where the carpenters made man
And the animals and birds,
Made all that lives,
The house to which man goes when he dies.

The sun is the chief's canoe.

*Bella Coola*
BRITISH COLUMBIA

First Man and First Woman
Made the mountains;
Fastened them with bolts of lightning
And sunbeams
And rainbows.

Made headdresses for them
Of pigeon feathers,
The feathers of bluebirds
And blackbirds and yellow warblers.

Wrapped them in cloud blankets
Blue and yellow and white and black.
Adorned them with crystal beads
And turquoise and jet
And haliotis shell.

In the beginning
First Man and First Woman
Made the mountains.

*Zuñi*
NEW MEXICO

The stars are night birds with bright breasts
Like hummingbirds.

Twinkling stars are birds flying slowly.
Shooting stars are birds darting swiftly.

*Taos Pueblo*
NEW MEXICO

North Wind dresses her daughter winds
In sparkling clothing.

East Wind's daughters are jealous.
They melt the snow-fur blankets.
They tear the icicle pendants.
They tangle the frost-feather headdresses

*Tlingit*
ALASKA

Until North Wind's daughters hide
Weeping, in their mother's lodge.

The northern lights are the flames
  and the smoke
From the fires of the dwarfs
Cooking seal and walrus meat.

*Makah*
CAPE FLATTERY,
BRITISH COLUMBIA

*Skidi Pawnee*
NEBRASKA

Lightning is a great giant
Who makes a path through the sky
For the thunderstorm.

His bonnet is feathered clouds.
His blanket is a black cloud.
His moccasins are the swift winds.

He carries the whirlwind like a sack
  slung over his shoulder.
He whips the clouds with his lariat.

Flint Boy tied his dog,
Left him shut in the lodge when he went hunting.

Flint Boy's wife untied the dog,
Let him leave the lodge because he barked,
Wanting to go hunting.

Flint Boy's dog ran up the mountain,
Called clouds to come for him,
Climbed on the back of a storm cloud,
Wrapped himself in a black cloud,
Went away because Flint Boy would not
    take him hunting.

Thunder is Flint Boy's dog
Barking.

*Yana*
CALIFORNIA

The winds are people dwelling
North, south;
Spirits, guarding the four corners of the sky.
They are the breathing of a monstrous white cow.
They are made by birds flying,
By Coyote and Deer racing.

South Wind is Doe starting up from her drinking,
Moving swiftly from the brook,
Softly through the meadow
Into the shaded wood,
Hurrying to her fawn.

East Wind is Moose running,
Rushing, stamping about,
Breathing in wet gusts.

North Wind is Bear prowling,
Climbing the long house roof,
Uncovering the smoke holes,
Reaching down with cold paws
To scatter the fires.

West Wind is Panther whining,
Angry, threatening Bobcat and Lynx,
Spoiling for a fight.
West Wind is Panther whining.

*Iroquois*
NEW YORK

Springs do not freeze in the cold of winter.

They bubble up through the snow

And no ice forms on them,

For their water comes up from the Land of the Ghosts

Below, where men speak only in yawns

And canoes are without bottoms

And winter never comes.

*Bella Coola*
BRITISH COLUMBIA

Winter is an old man walking in the woods.
He raps the trees with his war club,
And men in their lodges hear the sharp
  cracking blows.

*Iroquois*
NEW YORK

Icicles are the walking sticks of the winter winds.

*Bella Coola*
BRITISH COLUMBIA

Glooscap's wigwam
Once stood with the wigwams of men,
And men learned from him
How to raise corn, how to fish,
How to fashion bows and arrows
And to hunt with them.
They learned about the stars.
Whatever they needed to know,
Glooscap taught men.

Then he moved his wigwam
Far away beyond a high mountain
On a road guarded by serpents
And hidden by clouds.

But men know they have nothing to fear
When they see the rainbow:
Glooscap is home in his wigwam;
He is watching the homes of men.
He has hung up his packstrap as a sign.

*Micmac*
NEW BRUNSWICK
AND NOVA SCOTIA

*Crow*
GREAT PLAINS

The sun is a yellow-tipped porcupine
Lolloping through the sky,
Nibbling treetops and grasses and weeds,
Floating on rivers and ponds,
Casting shining barbed quills at the earth.

NATALIA BELTING is an associate professor of history at the University of Illinois, where she received her undergraduate and graduate degrees. Miss Belting's historical research has resulted in numerous books for young people, told in free-flowing poetic imagery. The list includes *Calendar Moon* (an ALA Notable Book), *The Sun Is a Golden Earring* (a Caldecott Medal Honor Book), and two Dutton titles, *The Land of the Taffeta Dawn* and *Our Fathers Had Powerful Songs*, the latter a collection of Indian song lore.

LEO and DIANE DILLON have worked as a husband-and-wife illustrating team for a number of years. They studied at the Parsons School of Design and the School of Visual Arts. The Dillons drew upon research materials to create the decorative motifs of the Indian nations in *Whirlwind Is a Ghost Dancing*. Among their recently illustrated titles are *The Ring in the Prairie* and *Behind the Back of the Mountain* (an ALA Notable Book). The Dillons live in Brooklyn, New York, with their son.

The display type is set in Palatino and the text type in Patina. The full-color art was drawn with pastels and acrylics in combination with a glaze. The book was printed at Universal Printing Company.